BY JONNY ZUCKER

ILLUSTRATED BY PAUL SAVAGE

Librarian Reviewer
Joanne Bongaarts
Educational Consultant
MS in Library Media Education, Minnesota State University, Mankato
Teacher and Media Specialist with Edina Public Schools, MN, 1993–2000

Reading Consultant
Elizabeth Stedem
Educator/Consultant, Colorado Springs, CO
MA in Elementary Education, University of Denver, CO

STONE ARCH BOOKS
Minneapolis   San Diego

First published in the United States in 2007
by Stone Arch Books,
151 Good Counsel Drive, P.O. Box 669,
Mankato, Minnesota 56002.
www.stonearchbooks.com

Originally published in Great Britain in 2003
by Badger Publishing Ltd.

Original work copyright © 2003 Badger Publishing Ltd
Text copyright © 2003 Jonny Zucker

The right of Jonny Zucker to be identified as the author
of this work has been asserted by him in accordance
with the Copyright, Designs and Patent Act 1988.

Library of Congress Cataloging-in-Publication Data
Zucker, Jonny.
   The Bombed House / by Jonny Zucker; illustrated by Paul Savage.
   p. cm. — (Keystone Books)
   Summary: During the German bombing of London in 1941, two
brothers see something strange in the rubble of a neighbor's house, but no
one believes them.
   ISBN-13: 978-1-59889-092-1 (hardcover)
   ISBN-10: 1-59889-092-1 (hardcover)
   ISBN-13: 978-1-59889-248-2 (paperback)
   ISBN-10: 1-59889-248-7 (paperback)
   1. London (England)—History—Bombardment, 1940–1941—Juvenile
fiction. [1. London (England)—History—Bombardment, 1940–1941—
Fiction. 2. World War, 1939–1945—Great Britain—Fiction.] I. Savage, Paul,
1971– ill. II. Title. III. Series: Keystone books (Stone Arch)
PZ7.Z77925Bo 2007
[Fic]—dc22   2006004056

1 2 3 4 5 6 11 10 09 08 07 06

Printed in the United States of America

TABLE OF CONTENTS

CHAPTER 1
NUMBER 46

January, 1941. The middle of World War II. German planes had been bombing the city of London for weeks.

Ned and Harry Jennings were running down Willow Street kicking a ball. Their house, number 27, was okay, but many of the houses on the street had been smashed to pieces.

Most of their friends had been sent to live with families in the country.

Some hadn't been so lucky.

Like their best friend, Charlie Smith, from number 33. He had died three months ago, along with all of his family, when a German bomb hit their house.

A family hadn't been found yet for Ned and Harry to stay with, so they were still in the city.

Waiting.

They stopped outside number 46 on Willow Street.

The top half of the house had been blasted off. So it just stood there, half of a house.

The owners, Mr. and Mrs. Young, were safe. They were staying down on the coast with friends.

Harry bent down to look in the rubble lying in the street, but Ned walked closer to the house.

He was looking in one of the windows when he heard a noise coming from inside.

It sounded like a groan.

"Harry," he called, "I heard a noise in there."

Harry stood up and looked at him.

"Don't be silly, Ned," he answered, checking his watch. "There's nothing there, and anyway, we need to get home."

They started to walk back toward their house.

Ned looked back at number 46.

He knew he wasn't wrong.

CHAPTER 2
DAD'S ORDERS

The next day, Ned told Harry he was going to say something about number 46 to their dad. Mr. Jennings was a member of the Home Guard, in charge of safety on Willow Street.

"I'll mention it at dinner," said Ned.

"Don't bother," said Harry. "You're making a big deal about nothing."

Ned did talk about it that evening.

Their dad tapped his fingers on the kitchen table after Ned told him about number 46.

"Listen, Ned," he began, "I know you mean well, but there are far more important things happening at the moment than your adventure games."

"There are German bombers flying over London every day. One plane was shot down last week only about a mile away from here," their dad said.

"Dad, I did hear something," claimed Ned.

Mrs. Jennings held up her hand.

"Maybe he's right, Bill," she said softly. "Maybe the Home Guard should have a look around number 46."

"All right, all right," replied Mr. Jennings to his wife.

"I'll get some of the guys to check it out," he added, "but I don't want you two going anywhere near that house. It's a death trap. Do you hear me?"

They both nodded.

"Okay," said Mr. Jennings. "Now can we keep eating our dinner?"

The Jennings family continued eating. Suddenly, the booming noise of the air-raid siren sounded.

They all stood up at once. They were used to hearing the sirens.

"Don't forget your gas masks, boys," called Mrs. Jennings.

The four of them ran out of the house and down the street to the safe air-raid shelter on the corner.

CHAPTER 3
FACE AT THE WINDOW

On Saturday, Ned and Harry went to their Aunt Rose's for lunch.

Aunt Rose told great stories about her childhood in Scotland, and she made good use of her rations to make really good meals.

They left her house as it was getting dark and walked home quickly.

As they were passing number 46 Willow Street, they both looked at its gloomy front.

Then, from inside the house, a pale face appeared at one of the windows.

It was there for a split second, and then it vanished. They both saw it.

"Ned, you were right!" whispered Harry. "There's someone in there. We've got to find out who it is."

Slowly, they walked up to the front door. Harry leaned forward to push it open.

They walked into the dark hallway.

They had only taken a few steps when part of the roof started to cave in. Rubble came crashing down.

They turned back and ran from the house, watching as more of the roof tumbled down.

"We were lucky not to be buried alive!" said Ned.

They ran home and burst through the front door.

Their mom and dad were in the kitchen having a cup of tea.

"We saw a face in the window of number 46!" shouted Harry.

"We went inside to look, but part of the roof fell in," added Ned.

"You did what?" demanded their father. He looked very angry. "You could have gotten yourselves killed!" he barked at them. "I told you to stay away from there!"

"We saw someone. We both did!" insisted Ned.

"Stop this nonsense!" commanded Mr. Jennings. "For your information, I had two of the Home Guard guys take a look around in there this afternoon."

"They found nothing at all. Did you hear me? Nothing," said their dad.

"Dad . . . ," said Ned.

"Dad nothing," replied Mr. Jennings. "Number 46 is totally off limits for both of you. The matter is closed, and that's final!"

CHAPTER 4
FOLLOW DANGER

Ned and Harry sat in their bedroom. They were sure they had seen a face at the window. Their dad just hadn't wanted to listen, and the Home Guard had checked out the place.

Their mom knocked on the door and came in.

She sat down on Harry's bed with them.

"Look, boys," she started, "your dad's not really angry with you. He just doesn't want you getting into any sort of danger. We know you want to help out, but it's very easy to imagine things in the middle of a war."

Ned was about to say something, but Harry shook his head.

Ned said nothing.

Their mom talked with them for a few more minutes and then left the room.

"I'm sorry I didn't believe you at first," said Harry.

"It's okay, don't worry," replied Ned.

"There's something weird going on at number 46," Harry said quietly.

"Dad said to stay away from it," said Ned.

"It doesn't matter what Dad said," whispered Harry. "Dangerous or not, we're going in there to find out what's going on."

CHAPTER 5
NIGHT MOVES

Early the next morning there was a knock on their front door.

It was a woman with some papers. She sat in the kitchen with Mr. and Mrs. Jennings.

Ned and Harry walked in.

"What's going on?" asked Ned.

"This is Mrs. Thornton," their mom explained.

"They've found a family for you to stay with in the Lake District," said their dad. "Mrs. Thornton has all of the paperwork for your move. You'll be staying with the Robinsons. And you'll leave early tomorrow morning."

Ned flashed a look at Harry.

For the whole day, their dad watched them like a hawk. "I only want you in the backyard or inside," he said.

As soon as it got dark, he told them to get ready for bed.

Ned started to complain but Mr. Jennings wouldn't listen.

"You have to leave early in the morning. I have Home Guard duty tonight," he said sternly.

"And I don't want you giving your mom any trouble," he added.

They went up to their bedroom and sat quietly.

Twenty minutes later they heard their dad saying goodbye to their mom and leaving the house.

Mrs. Jennings turned on the radio in the kitchen. The boys could hear the low hum of a war news report.

They turned off their bedroom light and waited for half an hour. Then Harry carefully slid open their bedroom window.

He looked at Ned.

Ned nodded.

As quietly as they could, they climbed out of the window, slid down the drainpipe, and landed on the ground at the front of the house.

The noise of the radio hummed from the kitchen.

They looked around them in the darkness. There was no one to be seen.

They stepped out onto the street.

CHAPTER 6
A SHOT IN THE DARK

Willow Street was completely dark because of the blackout.

After a few minutes, their eyes got used to the darkness, and they found number 46.

Creeping silently, they stepped over the rubble and into the house.

The hallway was covered with fallen bricks and pieces of broken wood.

Harry pulled a flashlight out of his pocket and turned it on.

They walked into the kitchen. Harry shined the light. Nothing was there.

They looked in the living room. Nothing.

The bathroom. Nothing.

"Maybe Dad was right after all," muttered Ned.

Then Harry shined his light down the steps that led to the cellar.

As he moved the light from left to right, something suddenly gleamed in its light. It was a black cross.

"Did you see that?" whispered Harry.

Without warning, the sound of a gunshot filled the air, and a bullet went whizzing past them.

Seconds later, they heard another gunshot, and Ned felt an incredibly sharp pain in his left arm.

He stumbled and fell forward down the cellar steps.

Harry called out and jumped down after him.

CHAPTER 7
CAPTURE

There were voices everywhere.

One of the voices was their dad's.

He and other members of the Home Guard dashed into the house and down the cellar steps.

Ned had been shot in the arm and had discovered a German soldier.

Harry was sitting on the soldier's back. The soldier was holding a gun.

The Home Guards jumped onto
the soldier and held him down.

The soldier screamed at them
in German.

Mr. Jennings and some of the
other Home Guards had a whispered
conversation, and then the German
soldier was dragged away, kicking
and screaming.

Mr. Jennings shined a flashlight onto Ned's arm.

"You're very lucky," he said quietly. "It's not too bad, but we'll need to get you to a hospital tonight. We'll go home first quickly and tell your mom what's going on."

The three of them walked up the cellar steps and out of the house to the pitch-black street.

"You've just given me the scare of my life," said Mr. Jennings slowly. "I know you disobeyed me, but I'm really proud of you."

"I'm sorry for not listening to you," he added. "Two guys from the Home Guard checked out the house, but they did it very quickly."

"They didn't search the cellar," he said. "It's my fault. I told them just to have a quick look."

"What were you whispering to those other Home Guards about?" asked Harry.

"We were talking about the German soldier," explained Mr. Jennings. "We think he's the pilot of the plane that was shot down last week. He must have found his way to number 46 and been hiding out there ever since."

"What will they do with him?" asked Harry.

"He'll be handed over to the army and become a prisoner of war," replied Mr. Jennings.

"Do you think we'll still be going to the country tomorrow?" asked Ned.

"If the hospital tells us you are okay, son, you'll both be on that train in the morning," said Mr. Jennings. "It isn't safe here in the city."

They reached their house.

Mrs. Jennings was standing on the doorstep, looking frantic with worry.

"I heard gunshots," she whispered. "What's going on, Bill? And what are you two doing out on the street?"

"It's nothing to worry about," Mr. Jennings replied. "Ned and Harry just need to get their coats for the walk to the hospital."

"Hospital?" asked Mrs. Jennings, with fear in her voice.

"It's Ned's arm," explained Mr. Jennings.

He put his arm around his wife's shoulders. "I'll explain it all to you on the way there," Mr. Jennings added. "He'll be completely fine."

Mr. Jennings gazed up into the night sky and saw Ned and Harry's bedroom window.

It was wide open.

He looked slowly from the window to his sons.

"Next time, please use the front door," he said with a smile.

ABOUT THE AUTHOR

Even as a child, Jonny Zucker wanted to be a writer. Today, he has written more than 30 books. He has also spent time working as a teacher, song writer, and stand-up comedian. Jonny lives in London with his wife and two children.

ABOUT THE ILLUSTRATOR

Paul Savage works in a design studio. He says illustrating books is "the best job." He's always been interested in illustrating books, and he loves reading. Paul also enjoys playing sports and running.

He lives in England with his wife and daughter, Amelia.

GLOSSARY

air raid (air rayd)—an attack by military aircraft, armed with bombs and rockets

blackout (BLAK out)—turning off lights in a city that might be visible to enemy aircraft during an air raid

coast (kohst)—land near the sea.

death trap (deth trap)—an unsafe building

gas mask (gass mask)—a mask that protects the face and lungs from poisonous gas or other harmful substances

Home Guard (home gard)—a volunteer group formed to defend a city or country while the regular army is fighting somewhere else

rations (RASH-uns)—a set amount of food given to people when food is scarce, as in a war

rubble (RUH-buhl)—broken pieces of hard materials, such as stone

sternly (STURN-lee)—strictly, firmly

DISCUSSION QUESTIONS

1. What do you know about World War II? Explain and talk about it.

2. This story relates very dangerous events, but is told in a matter-of-fact way. How do you think each of the characters — Ned, Harry, Mr. Jennings, and Mrs. Jennings — feel about what happens in this story? How would you feel? Explain your answers.

3. Did the boys do the right thing by sneaking out and going to number 46? Why or why not?

WRITING PROMPTS

1. Mr. Jennings is a member of the Home Guard, and is supposed to keep the neighborhood safe. How does he keep his own family safe? What might he have done differently?

2. What will happen next to Harry and Ned when they stay with the new family in the Lake District? Will they get into new adventures? Write a continuation of the story.

3. What kind of picture do you have in your head about the neighborhood in this story and all that is going on because of the war? Write a description of what you think it would be like to live on Ned and Harry's street.

ALSO BY JONNY ZUCKER

Alien Abduction

When Shelly and Dan are abducted by Zot the alien, they teach him about the ways of earthling teenagers. Hopefully they can convince Mr. Tann of their story before they end up in big trouble!

Skateboard Power

Nick Jones was all set to win the skateboard competition — until the bully, Dan Abbot, stepped in and ruined his chances. With no board, Nick has no hope. Time is running out.

OTHER BOOKS
IN THIS SET

Sleepwalker
by J. Powell

When Josh decides to follow Tom one night on one of his sleepwalking adventures, real life suddenly turns into a nightmare!

Space Games
by David Orme

Todd's travels across the universe are no match for a good game of soccer. When a soccer field is built aboard his starship, he dreams of leading his team to universal glory.

INTERNET SITES

Do you want to know more about subjects related to this book? Or are you interested in learning about other topics? Then check out FactHound, a fun, easy way to find Internet sites.

Our investigative staff has already sniffed out great sites for you!

Here's how to use FactHound:

1. Visit *www.facthound.com*

2. Select your grade level.

3. To learn more about subjects related to this book, type in the book's ISBN number: **1598890921**.

4. Click the **Fetch It** button.

FactHound will fetch the best Internet sites for you!